INDIAN TWO FEET
and the
GRIZZLY BEAR

by Margaret Friskey

illustrated by John Hawkinson

CHILDRENS PRESS, CHICAGO

Library of Congress Cataloging in Publication Data

Friskey, Margaret, 1901—
  Indian Two Feet and the grizzly bear.

  SUMMARY: An Indian boy tries to awaken a sleeping
bear because he wants its furry skin to warm him
during the cold winter.
  [1. Indians—Fiction] I. Hawkinson, John,
1912—   illus. II. Title.
PZ7.F918Ip4   [E]   74-7481
ISBN 0-516-03508-8

3 4 5 6 7 8 9 10 11 12 13 14 15 16 17 18 19 20 21 22 23 24 25 R 79 78 77 76

"I want a big,
thick, warm, furry
robe for my bed," said
Indian Two Feet.
"The wind is cold.
Snow will come."

"Make a big,
thick, warm, furry
robe for your bed,"
said his father.
"You will need
the skins of TEN
squirrels,

or NINE rabbit skins,
or EIGHT possum skins,

or SEVEN beaver skins,
or SIX raccoon skins,

or FIVE wild cat skins,
or FOUR fox skins,

or THREE wolf skins,

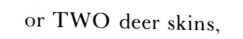

or TWO deer skins,

or just ONE big
thick, warm, furry
skin of a grizzly bear."

"A grizzly bear
sleeps in the cave
in the hill," said
Indian Two Feet.

"He may sleep
all winter in his
big, thick, warm
furry skin," said
his father.

Indian Two Feet
rode to the cave.
He took his drum.

"I will scare
that grizzly bear.
I will wake him up,"
he said.

15

He stopped at
the cave.
He pounded on
his drum. BANG!
Thump, thump, thump.
BANG!
Thump, thump, thump.
The bear did not wake up.

"You foolish
little Indian,"
said his father.
"A little Indian
does not scare
a great big, furry
grizzly bear."

The next day
Indian Two Feet
rode to the cave.

He took a bowl
of honey.

A hungry bear
would smell the
honey. He would
wake up.

But the bear
did not smell
the honey.

Two raccoons
licked the bowl
clean.

The next day,
Indian Two Feet
caught some fish.

He rode toward the
cave with a big
string of fish.

The bear was
not there. He
had come out to
look for food.
He smelled the
fish. He followed
Indian Two Feet.

He got closer,
and closer,
and closer!

Suddenly, the bear
jumped. He grabbed
the fish. He ran
into the cave.
He ate the fish.

Indian Two Feet
rode home.
He was sad.
He knew now
that grizzly bear
would sleep all
winter in his big,
thick, warm, furry
skin.

That night
Indian Two Feet
saw a big, thick,
warm, woolly blanket
on his bed.

His mother had
made it.

"Sleep well, little
Two Feet," said his
father.

"When you are bigger,
you can catch a
grizzly bear."

About the Author:

Margaret Friskey, Editor Emeritus of Childrens Press, was Editor-in-Chief of the company from its conception in 1945 until her retirement in 1971. It was under her editorial direction that Childrens Press expanded to become a major juvenile publishing house. Although she now has more free time, her days are by no means quiet. She spends time with her children and grandchildren, all of whom live near enough to her little house in Evanston to visit often. She also has more time to concentrate on her writing.

About the Artist:

John Hawkinson lives in the country with his two daughters, three horses, two goats, a dog and a part-time cat. The horses cut the grass and haul manure and wood. The goats give milk and the dog takes care of things when the family is gone. John and his daughters saw firewood, grind wheat, pick wild greens, fish, ski, swim, garden, ride, dance, paint, make movies, sew, canoe, listen to the birds and wait for each new season. They have two acres, no money and a good life.